Baseball
ODDITIES

Baseball
ODDITIES
BIZARRE PLAYS &
OTHER FUNNY STUFF

Wayne Stewart
Illustrated by Matt LaFleur

Best Wishes,
Wayne Stewart

Sterling Publishing Co., Inc.
New York

I dedicate this, my first book, to five of the people I love: my father, the late Owen (O.J.) Stewart, who taught me to love words; my mother Margaret, who taught me to love reading; and to my wife Nancy and sons Sean and Scott.

Library of Congress Cataloging-in-Publication Data
Stewart, Wayne, 1951-
    Baseball oddities:bizarre plays & other funny stuff/
Stewart ; illustrated by Matt LaFleur.
      p. cm.
    Includes index.
    ISBN 0-8069-0709-6
    1. Baseball--Anecdotes. 2. Baseball--Miscellanea. I Title
GV873.S84 1998
796.357--dc21

                               97-44350
                               CIP

10 9 8 7 6 5 4 3 2

First paperback edition published in 1999 by
Sterling Publishing Company, Inc.
387 Park Avenue South, New York, N.Y. 10016
© 1998 by Wayne Stewart
Distributed in Canada by Sterling Publishing
% Canadian Manda Group, One Atlantic Avenue, Suite 105
Toronto, Ontario, Canada M6K 3E7
Distributed in Great Britain and Europe by Chris Lloyd
463 Ashley Road, Parkstone Poole, Dorset BH14 0AX, England
Distributed in Australia by Capricorn Link (Australia) Pty Ltd.
P.O. Box 6651, Baulkham Hills, Business Centre, NSW 2153, Australia
Manufactured in the United States of America
All rights reserved
Sterling ISBN 0-8069-0709-6 Trade
                0-8069-1895-0 Paper

TABLE OF CONTENTS

INTRODUCTION

Lately, it's become fashionable to bash the game of baseball. Critics point to the greed of players and owners alike as being the main cause for the ruination of the game. There's no loyalty towards the fans any longer, they contend. Furthermore, the baseball strikes (as in work stoppages, not balls and strikes) have also made fans cynical.

Some feel the game is suffering through a very rapid and precipitous decline, in which it has been transformed from being the national pastime to a moribund state. They contrast the condition of the game today to its popularity during the "Golden Years." Interestingly, that era is often considered to be any time frame in which the critic grew up—be it the Babe Ruth years (the 1920s and the 1930s) or the decades of such superstars as Willie Mays, Hank Aaron, Ernie Banks, Mickey Mantle (the 1950s-1970s). Such a comparison is bound to lead to the conclusion that the "good ol' days" are dead.

However, these pessimists are forgetting one thing: baseball, despite its shortcomings, is still a fun game. It's a game which has more than its share of oddities—of wild and interesting characters; of bizarre plays and crazy coincidences; of witty quotes and unmatched humor.

So, forget the negatives and blot out the much-criticized mercenary facets of the game. Here's a look at the other side of the sport, the part that made us fall in love with this wonderful game in the first place. So, sit back, relax, and enjoy.

Wayne Stewart

BASEBALL IN THE 1990s: STILL HUMOR IN THE GAME

Humor Endures

For those who think the game of baseball has become strictly a humorless business, think again. True, a person would be naive not to realize baseball is a big business and players are indeed earning astronomical sums of money. However, a quick look around a clubhouse or dugout during a baseball season will reveal that players nowadays are laughing and enjoying themselves perhaps as much as players of any era. If a skeptic needs evidence to support this contention, just consider the following anecdotes.

Alexander the Great

Early in the 1996 season, the Texas Rangers crushed the Baltimore Orioles by a score of 26-7, with all of the 26 runs being earned. In the eighth inning alone, the Rangers scored 16 times as Oriole pitching dished up 99 juicy pitches to the salivating sluggers during the seemingly endless frame.

Desperate for another pitcher, Baltimore took utility infielder Manny Alexander off the bench and put him out on the mound. He gave up four walks and a grand slam while toiling just two-thirds of an inning.

That prompted Orioles announcer and ex-pitcher Mike Flanagan to deadpan, "There are some great pitching Alexanders in baseball history: Grover Cleveland Alexander, Doyle Alexander, and now, Manny Alexander."

Brushback Time

When Roger Clemens and Jose Canseco became teammates as members of the Boston Red Sox (1995-96), it ended years of competition as fierce opponents. The two stars had battled each other many times; now they would work together.

Clemens smiled recalling the first time he pitched batting practice to Canseco in spring training as teammates. "When Jose stepped in, I said, 'I can't believe it. I've got

HEY! I'M ON YOUR TEAM NOW!

to sit here and throw you balls down the middle?' I threw the first couple of balls up under his arms. You just can't break old habits."

An Appeal to an Agent

While players' agents have reputations for being ruthless and greedy, they can also be reasoned with. For example, Lou Piniella, manager of the Seattle Mariners, tells a story about such an agent.

It seems one of the Mariners wasn't getting much playing time. Obviously the player's agent wanted his man on the field where he would have a chance to produce impressive statistics and thus earn more money. It was also obvious, from Piniella's point of view, that he couldn't play someone who was not performing well at the time. So when Piniella was faced with the rather irate agent who was demanding more playing time, the skipper had to be clever and somewhat diplomatic.

Piniella said, "I'd ask him, 'Do you like your job?' " The agent was no doubt quite puzzled at this seemingly evasive opening gambit, but replied, "Yes."

At that point Piniella came back with, "Well, I like my job, too, and I'm not going to keep it long if I keep playing your client." His tactic has worked more than once apparently, because Piniella concluded his tale by saying, "I don't get many calls from agents any more."

Poor Choice of Words

The Minnesota Twins began the 1996 season by undertaking a bold experiment. In Rick Aguilera, they possessed one of the best relief pitchers in all of baseball, a highly valuable commodity. They decided to try converting him into a starting pitcher, instead of continuing his normal role of being their "closer."

After working the first three innings of an early spring training game, Aguilera made his way to the clubhouse. As the game's starter, he had got in some light work and was through for the day.

He quickly showered and was ready to leave the ballpark even though the game was still in progress. Since he had usually worked the last inning of many of the Twins contests, it felt odd to be dressed and ready to depart while being in an empty locker room.

He commented later of that peculiar sensation by saying, "I hope I don't shower alone many times during the season. I hope I'll be showering with the boys after (successfully giving his team) a long start."

Now, while a baseball fan knew what Aguilera meant, it was also clear that the quote sounded a bit odd, to say the least.

No Security

Prior to capturing the 1996 World Series as the manager of the New York Yankees, Joe Torre had to realize his job was not exactly secure. First of all, his boss and Yankee owner, George Steinbrenner, has a reputation for firing managers with the frequency of most people changing their underwear. Secondly, no manager ever totally enjoys job security.

With all that in mind, when Torre was asked (before his World Series success) for his views on a plan to move Yankee Stadium to Manhattan in the year 2002, he was wise enough to know a manager can't plan too far ahead. He replied with a grim sense of humor, "To be honest, it's not really my concern. You're talking to a guy with a two-year contract." By the way, for now at least, both Torre and Yankee Stadium are still in the Bronx.

It's All in How You Interpret Things

In the spring of 1994, there was a great deal of talk about a rather unusual situation facing the Los Angeles Dodgers. They had a rookie pitcher named Chan Ho Park who was from Korea. Since he spoke no English, the big question was whether the pitching coach would be able to communicate with him while making a mound visit during a game. Since baseball officials had ruled Park's interpreter couldn't go along for the conference on the hill, this was a very real concern.

Upon hearing all of the fuss, Graig Nettles, always noted for his humor, came up with a great quip. "I don't know what all this concern about the interpreter is all about," he opined. "George Scott (former Red Sox player) played 15 years and he never had an interpreter." Scott, hardly known for his oratory skills or his dazzling articulation, probably was the only one who didn't enjoy Nettles's wit.

Strike One

When the players' strike of 1994 took place, few people were happy about the state of the game. Even through this difficult situation, though, humor endured. For example, there was the time in March of 1995 when a bitter fan attended a Pittsburgh versus Minnesota exhibition contest. At that time, baseball was trying to use replacement players rather than cave in to the regular players' requests. The spectator gazed down on the field and spotted a rather portly, somewhat disheveled man. Angrily the fan bellowed, "Look at you—you're a disgrace. You're not a player."

Ironically, and humorously, he was totally correct—the man he was degrading was Pirate coach Tommy Sandt.

Strike Two

In 1994, Cleveland Indians General Manager John Hart came up with a good line concerning the striking players. He was asked if he felt that the regular players would picket the "replacement" spring training games. "Personally, I think it's a stretch for union members whose average salary is $1.2 million to be out there. And can you see Cecil Fielder walking around camp wearing a sandwich board?" Since Fielder goes 250 pounds (or more—the 250 is what was listed in the team roster guide), the answer to Hart's question is, "No, it's unfathomable to picture Fielder parading around in such an outfit."

Strike Three

New York Yankee broadcaster Mike Kay was working a "replacement" game between the Yanks and the Boston Red Sox. Kay began reviewing a play in the typical fashion of all baseball announcers, but then added a twist. "For those of you scoring at home," he said, "you really ought to get some help."

Mr. Replacement

Alan Cockrell was a 32-year-old player who had kicked around in many teams' minor league systems as the 1995 season began. In fact, he had logged 1,199 pro games, of which none took place at the major league level.

The Colorado Rockies were in need of replacement players to start the season. When Cockrell learned he was being considered by Colorado, he was asked if he felt he could handle the situation. He summed up his situation by saying, "When you look at the replacement guys, I not only fit the mold, I am mold."

Wishing He Wasn't Made of Iron

In 1995, the one event that helped baseball regain some of its lost luster due to the strike was Cal Ripken's record-breaking performance. It was then that this iron-man broke Lou Gehrig's streak of having played in 2,130 consecutive contests.

In April of that year, before he snapped the mark, Ripken and his Orioles were playing the Kansas City Royals. Tom Goodwin of the Royals was robbed of a hit by super-shortstop Ripken early in the game. Later, the durable Ripken tagged Goodwin out on an attempted steal.

Those plays prompted Goodwin to later say, "I wasn't too thrilled when he made that play or when he tagged me out. I was thinking, 'Why doesn't he take a day off?'" Not likely. As of 1997, Ripken was still playing daily, although at third base, not shortstop.

Pitcher Turned Slugger

When the 1997 season opened, Chicago Cubs center fielder Brian McRae felt safe concerning a promise he had made three years earlier. He had told teammate Frank Castillo he would buy him a Mercedes Benz if Castillo, a pitcher and notoriously poor hitter, could ever swat a home run (even during batting practice).

Well, on May 30th Castillo, a .108 hitter, went deep twice during his rounds in the batting cage prior to a game. This hitting display pleased the man who normally couldn't hit a lick, but brought dismay and utter disbelief to McRae. When asked what he made of the whole situation, McRae simply stated, "He's still the worst hitting pitcher I've ever seen!"

ODD BASEBALL PLAYS

Mulholland's Mitt Magic

After watching baseball for decades, many fans come to believe that they've seen it all. In reality, the nature of baseball is such that about the time you become blasé, something odd will come along to make you shout, "Wow!"

One such play occurred on September 3, 1986, when a San Francisco Giants rookie pitcher named Terry Mulholland made an amazing fielding play. He was facing the New York Mets in the third inning when he

stabbed a hard grounder off the bat of Keith Hernandez.

It turned out the Mets All Star had drilled the ball so hard, it became lodged in Mulholland's glove. The southpaw hurler tried to pull the ball loose, but he also realized time was running out, and Hernandez would soon reach base safely. So, he trotted a few strides towards first base, gave up on freeing the ball, removed his glove (the ball still nestled inside), and tossed the glove to the first baseman, Bob Brenly. The umpire didn't miss a beat as he correctly ruled that Hernandez was out in a truly bizarre play.

Optical Illusion

During a 1969 contest between the Atlanta Braves and the Houston Astros, a Houston base runner committed a terrible base blunder. His mistake was not due to disobeying a coach, being outwitted by an opponent, or being unaware of the game situation. Instead, his own faulty eyesight duped him.

It began with the runner taking a normal lead off third base. As the pitcher began his delivery, the runner danced down the baseline a few steps. Then, upon seeing the ball bounce wildly off the mitt of Atlanta catcher Bob Didier, the daring runner darted home. It's hard to say who was more astonished a few seconds later, the runner or the catcher, but both were clearly perplexed. The runner couldn't believe his eyes because there was Didier, still squatting at the plate with the ball in his mitt. Didier, who had certainly not missed the ball, was wondering why the runner would dash for the well-guarded home plate. Didier, however, was not so baffled that he didn't easily apply the tag for a ridiculously easy out.

The explanation? It turns out the runner had seen an object fly out of the catcher's glove. It seems Didier had been wearing a protective casing over a finger he had injured earlier. Since the casing was white, and since the impact of the ball meeting the mitt had caused it to soar towards the backstop, the runner had been deceived into thinking he could easily score. It was yet another odd and highly embarrassing baseball moment.

More Humiliation

Max West was playing for the Boston Red Sox when he perpetrated a strange faux pas. It started innocently enough when West was retired at first base on a routine groundout. On the play, a teammate advanced to third base. West trudged back to his dugout, and he apparently was extremely slow in doing so. As he was about to descend the steps and make his way to the bench, he spied a baseball.

He must have figured the ball had been fouled off by the next batter. So, as a friendly gesture, West stooped over, picked up the ball, and tossed it to the enemy catcher to save him a few steps.

But the ball had not been fouled off! It was in play, having escaped from the catcher after a pitch. In other words, it was a passed ball that would permit the runner off third to score. And, normally he would have scored with ease, but not when a teammate throws a perfect strike to the opposing catcher.

Needless to say, the runner was nailed at the plate. An official scorekeeper might even be tempted to teasingly give West an assist on the play. It's not quite certain what West's manager wanted to give him.

History in the Making

Babe Herman was one of baseball's zaniest players. His career, which spanned the years 1926-1945, is studded with odd plays. Most of those plays were due to his ineptitude. While he was a fine hitter (.324 lifetime), his attention to running and fielding skills was indifferent at best.

The most famous Herman tale has to be the time he hit a bases-loaded double which amazingly turned into a double play. To make matters worse, only one run scored on a play which should have probably, in fact, cleared the bases.

Herman's Brooklyn Dodgers were at the plate facing pitcher George Mogridge back on August 15, 1926, when he smacked a line drive off the right-field wall. Hank DeBerry scored easily from third base, of course.

The runner on second, a pitcher named Dazzy Vance, advanced to third, but didn't run full speed for the plate. Perhaps because he was a pitcher he wasn't very skilled on the base paths and, therefore, made this base-running blunder. He decided he wouldn't succeed in making it home, so he scooted back to third instead.

Meanwhile, the Dodger on first base, Chick Fewster, having a different angle on the play, realized the ball was going to drop in for a base hit. He, therefore, made a dash for third. When he saw Vance retreat to third, Fewster slowed down between second and third so he would be able to trot back to second if Vance stayed put at third.

This comedy of errors reached its climax when Herman, running full tilt with his head down, tried to stretch his hit into a triple. At that point, Fewster had to

continue to third base to prevent Herman from illegally passing him on the base path.

The end result was incredible—three men were all trying to occupy the same base! Eventually, two Dodgers were ruled out and Herman got credit for a double. In the process, he also gained instant baseball immortality for this remarkable gaff.

By the way, when the smoke cleared, it was Vance who was the only runner not declared out since he, as the lead runner, was entitled to stay at third. Only Fewster and Herman were ruled out. Hence, despite what some sources say, Herman did not triple into a triple play. Still, hitting a double that is turned into a double play is bad enough.

History Repeating

In 1997, history repeated itself when Cleveland's Matt Williams doubled into a peculiar double play. When Williams strode to the plate, Jim Thome, who had drawn a walk, was on first with one out. Williams tattooed a pitch off Seattle's Bob Wolcott. The ball ricocheted off the left-field wall for what Williams knew was a sure double. Thome was chugging hard as he rounded third base.

At the last second, Thome's third base coach thrust his hands up high, giving the signal for Thome to halt at third. Too late. The Mariners left fielder, Lec Tinsley, had quickly retrieved the ball and fired it back to the infield. Thome tried to scamper back to third, but was nailed as Russ Davis applied the tag.

In the meantime, Williams had seen Thome make the turn around third. Williams knew that if Thome raced for home plate the Mariners would throw the ball there and Williams could coast into third base. When the defense threw to third instead, Williams was trapped between second and third and was eventually tagged out after a rundown.

Keeping Up with the Joneses

Two weird plays occurred in two World Series separated by 12 years, but connected by one coincidence. During the 1957 series between the Milwaukee Braves and the New York Yankees, Nippy Jones appeared at the plate for the Braves. When he was hit on the foot by a pitch, he began to trot to first base as he was entitled to do.

However, the umpire didn't believe the ball had actually struck Jones. The ump felt the pitch had simply bounced off the dirt near home plate, so he ordered the batter back to the batter's box. Doing his best Perry Mason imitation, Jones retrieved Exhibit A, the ball, and showed a black smudge on the baseball. Convinced the mark was from the polish on Jones's shoe, the umpire finally awarded him first base.

Ironically, in the 1969 World Series involving the New York Mets and the Baltimore Orioles another player was hit on the foot. Once again, the batter claimed his right to go to first, and once more the umpire denied the claim.

Recalling the 1957 incident, the batter recreated the shoe polish scenario and won his plea, too. What makes this such an odds-defying event is the fact that the batter was also named Jones— Cleon in this case.

Just Like W.C. Fields

There's an old story about the last days in the life of comedian W.C. Fields. It seems that even though he was never a very religious person, he was seen reading a Bible on his deathbed. Confused at this sight, a friend gently asked Fields if this was a case of a dying man finding religion. Legend has it Fields gazed at his friend, and then replied in his famous drawl, "No, I'm merely looking for loopholes."

Don Hoak of the Pittsburgh Pirates is said to have searched for and actually found a gaping loophole in baseball's record book. During a game in the 1960s, he reached second base. The next batter hit a long foul ball down the left-field line. Since Hoak couldn't be certain at first if the ball might drop in fair territory, he ran full speed for third base.

When the third base coach told him to hold up, that the ball was indeed foul, Hoak slowed down. He did not, however, retrace his steps back to second base, as is the normal procedure. Instead, he stayed in his tracks just a few steps away from third.

The umpire was puzzled and asked Hoak what he was doing. Hoak replied, "I'm taking my lead." There was no rule saying he had to return to second, and there certainly was no rule limiting the lead a runner could take off a base.

Therefore, the pitcher was given the ball and told to resume play. When the pitcher toed the rubber to get his sign for the next pitch, Hoak simply took a large stride and reached third base. Officially he was awarded a stolen base. Unofficially, he could joke with teammates about the great jump he got. Finally, a rule was devised to prohibit such tactics ever again.

Hoak's ingenuity was reminiscent of a Bill Veeck line.

Famous for taking advantage of any weakness in the rulebook, Veeck once proclaimed, "I try not to break the rules, but merely to test their elasticity."

Bizarre Base Burglary

Contrary to a widely held belief, Herman "Germany" Schaefer was not the first man to "steal" first base. Still, his story is such a classic it is worth repeating as a sort of Ripley's Believe-It-or-Not play. In 1911, while playing for the Washington Senators, Schaefer was on first base while a teammate, Clyde Milan, was taking his lead off third. On the next pitch Schaefer took off for second, hoping to draw a throw from the catcher that might allow the runner from third to score. Instead of succeeding on this double steal, Schaefer was able to take second unimpeded, since the catcher offered no throw.

Undaunted, on the next pitch Schaefer scampered back to first base, and was again ignored by the catcher. That was fine with Schaefer, known to be a "clown prince" of baseball. In this case, however, he had more in mind that just foolery.

His plan was to retreat to that base in order to set up the double steal again. Of course, he wasn't officially credited with a steal of first, but it's said that he did rattle the pitcher.

So, on the very next pitch Schaefer again streaked for second. For the second time in a matter of moments he stole that base. It's almost enough to lead to a facetious search of the record books for an entry, "most times stealing the same base during one at bat, twice by Schaefer, 1911."

What's more, the runner from third finally did cross home in one of the game's most peculiar plays ever.

Needless to say, nowadays there is a rule forbidding such an event. The rulebook bans such tactics, as it makes a "travesty of the game."

The Case of the Disappearing Baseball

In 1958, Leon Wagner was a raw rookie for the San Francisco Giants. During a July 1st contest, the opposing Chicago Cubs took advantage of his inexperience. Cubs' batter Tony Taylor hit a shot to left field, where Wagner was stationed.

The ball bounded into the Cubs' bullpen before Wagner could track it down. He did notice, though, that the relief pitchers, who were viewing the game from that location, scattered. When those relievers stared under their bench, Wagner knew the ball had come to rest there.

He was wrong. He had been fooled by the enemy, who realized the ball had actually gone beyond the bullpen. In truth, the ball had come to a stop about 45 feet further down the foul line. It was nestled in a rain gutter. By the time Wagner understood he had been faked out, Taylor had breezed around the bases for one of the oddest inside-the-park homers ever.

Disappearing Baseball, Part II

Larry Biittner was manning right field for the Cubs in a 1979 game against the New York Mets when another baseball performed a vanishing act. A low line drive off the bat of Bruce Boisclair came Biittner's way, but eluded his diving effort. He knew the ball had to be near him because he had deadened it when as it glanced off his

glove. So, he pounced off the turf and back to his feet, losing his hat during that motion.

He began looking around for the ball so the batter couldn't advance to second base. No matter how hard he looked, no matter in which direction he gazed, he could not find the ball. It took on comic proportions as the crowd roared with delight, even as Boisclair raced past second and on towards third.

About that time Biittner, like Wagner, finally figured it out. The ball had deflected off his glove and trickled under his cap. He had found it (as a cliché goes) in the last place he looked for it. Interestingly, his timing was perfect in that he was able to throw out the runner at third.

QUOTES OF THE GAME

Baseball "Poetry"

Over the years, the words spoken by baseball players have been carefully preserved as if they were precious lines from the mind of a poet. Ironically, most baseball quotes aren't meant to be taken so seriously. Still, many of the quotes are worth hearing, especially the ones that show some creativity and wit. Surprisingly, baseball's funny lines often are full of figurative and rich language.

Ron Luciano was a popular umpire—that in itself is unusual. The fact that he went on to write several books and become a television analyst after his umpiring days is revealing. Luciano loved a hearty laugh even more than making his flamboyant calls on the diamond. He injected his sense of humor into all facets of his life.

Later he became a television announcer, frequently covering games which were not being carried nationally. Thus his words spoken into a microphone would only get widespread attention if the nationally covered game were rained out. This seldom happened, making backup announcers feel their work wasn't gaining much recognition. It could truly be a bit frustrating.

Luciano colorfully summed it up saying, "Doing the television backup games is like doing a telethon for hiccups."

Figurative Language

Bobby Murcer, an outfielder for many years, also came up with a clever simile of his own. He was a fine hitter, but he couldn't stand trying to hit knuckleballs. That pitch is so unpredictable, nobody knows which way the ball will dart. Men who are power hitters and who love a diet of fastballs detest the elusive knuckleball.

A reporter asked Murcer what went through his mind when he had to face master knuckleball artist Phil Niekro. Murcer thought for a moment before coming up with, "Trying to hit him is like trying to eat Jell-O with chopsticks."

That's not unlike the quote attributed to pitcher Curt Simmons regarding the prospect of having to pitch to the great home-run hitter Hank Aaron. "Throwing a fastball by Aaron," said the hurler, "is like trying to sneak the sun past a rooster."

From the "Poetic" to the Absurd

When Bryan Harvey was pitching out of the California Angels bullpen, he was asked to list his lifetime dream. Harvey was apparently taking the question seriously (something ballplayers don't always do with such questions) as he stated, "Stop all the killing in the world."

While that was a fine sentiment, it somehow didn't mesh with his reply to a request to list his hobbies. His favorite pastimes were hunting and fishing. Quite an odd paradox!

Kiner-isms

One man famous, or infamous, for having an absurd way with words is New York Mets announcer Ralph Kiner. Here are a few of his gems:

* "All of Steve Bedrosian's saves have come in relief."
* When Kevin McReynolds was enjoying a great year for the Mets, Kiner informed his audience that McReynolds owned, "record-setting records."
* Kiner once imposed his wisdom that, "Third base is a reactionary position."
* Instead of identifying his show's sponsor as Manufacturer's Hanover, Kiner muffed the line from his "script" and called it "Manufacturer's Hangover."

More Absurdities

The phrase "play me or trade me" is an old baseball line. The player who mutters those words is a man who has been benched although he feels he should be playing. His ultimatum is blunt, implying he is certainly good enough to play elsewhere. It is a line reeking with self-confidence on the player's part.

Once, though, a marginal player named Chico Salmon confused his manager with this unique demand, "Bench me or keep me."

Then there was Dennis "Oil Can" Boyd, a pitcher who could rival anyone when it came to zany quotes. When he was with the Red Sox, there was a bomb threat made on a flight the team was about to take. A writer asked Boyd what he thought about the situation.

Boyd managed to came up with these cryptic observations: "I don't know anything about it. They keep me pretty much in the dark about these things. Even if it had blown up, I wouldn't have known anything about it."

The Subject Is Fans

Sometimes spectators let loose a stream of unpleasant words about players and/or a team's front office. However, at times baseball players and officials have had the last word.

For instance, big-league pitcher Bo Belinsky was disgusted with the infamous Philadelphia Phillies fans. According to Belinsky, those fans "would boo a funeral." It's been said they'd boo Santa Claus as well.

Los Angeles Dodger fans, on the other hand, have a different type of reputation. It has been said the fans will attend games in full force, but aren't too knowledgeable. They have also been accused of being guilty of paying more attention to scanning the throng to see what celebrities are in attendance than actually watching the game.

One Dodger official summed it up by saying, "In Los Angeles 20,000 people will show up at the park accidentally, just to see what the lights are about."

The New York Giants played in the Polo Grounds before their 1958 departure to San Francisco. In their final season in New York, they managed to win only 69 games while dropping 85 decisions. The fans weren't exactly packing the park. Even the last home game ever prior to the exodus couldn't draw a substantial crowd.

A Giants public relations man by the name of Garry Schumacher had the foresight, though, to realize, "If all the people who will claim in the future that they were here today had actually turned out, we wouldn't have to be moving in the first place."

Wonderful One-Liners

Chicago comedian Tom Dressen joked, "I grew up in an age when we used to pray the White Sox and Cubs would merge so Chicago would have only one bad team."

Towards the end of his illustrious career, pitcher Robin Roberts was asked to recall his greatest thrill during an All-Star game. He didn't hesitate at all. "When Mickey Mantle bunted with the wind blowing out in Crosley Field," he quipped.

Dave McNally was also a fine pitcher. Usually when he was on the hill he could depend on his third baseman, the legendary defensive whiz Brooks Robinson, to give him stellar glove support. At the start of the 1974 season, one of those freakish baseball streaks took place—

Robinson was guilty of committing three errors over the first eight Oriole games. McNally couldn't help but get in a verbal jab at Robinson. "You've gone from a human vacuum cleaner to a litterbug," he scolded.

More Comedic Lines

Speedy St. Louis Cardinals left fielder Lou Brock had just robbed the Pirates of a hit with a spectacular stab of a long drive. The Pirates manager, Bill Virdon, shook his head in utter disbelief. In spite of his agony, Virdon came up with this gem: "He could never make that play again...not even on instant replay."

Johnny Sain was not only a great pitcher, he later became a pitching guru, coaching many 20-game winners. He was frequently asked his opinion on the subject of pitchers' conditioning. Do they constantly need to run in order to get in shape and be effective, Sain was asked. He clearly didn't believe in miles and miles of running for his staff. As he put it, "You don't run the ball across the plate."

Luis Tiant, a standout pitcher who wasn't fond of all the sprints and laps his coaches had made him run over his long career, naturally sided with Sain. His logic was, "How many 20-game seasons has Jesse Owens got?"

Larceny in His Heart, Lead in His Feet

There are times in baseball when a slow-footed runner gets a burst of inspiration and tries to steal a base. Thanks to a lumbering runner named Ping Bodie, there's even an ancient baseball saying regarding such instances. After Bodie was gunned out by a mile trying to steal, a writer penned the now famous words, "He had larceny in his heart, but lead in his feet."

Larry Parrish, like Bodie, had spikes of lead. During his career, which spanned nearly 1,900 major league games, the good-hit, no-run Parrish pilfered a mere 30 bases. In 1994, he was the manager of the Detroit Tigers AAA minor league team in Toledo. Parrish had his team running at every opportunity. By the end of the year, Toledo led the International League in steals. Parrish explained the rather anomalous situation by saying with a grin, "I always knew how to steal, I just couldn't do it."

Superhuman Slugger

In 1993, Ken Griffey, Jr. of the Seattle Mariners was in the midst of an unbelievably torrid batting streak. By the time his blazing hot spell came to an end, he had homered in a record-tying eight consecutive ball games. Only Dale Long and Don Mattingly had ever achieved such a home run spree.

One of his blasts had come against the Cleveland Indians, who were managed by Mike Hargrove. When asked to comment on the Griffey poke, Hargrove shook his head and said, "He's so hot, he could hit a home run off Superman."

Sun Spots

In May of 1993, Hargrove's troops were playing Detroit. Rob Deer of the Tigers hit a ball to left field which many observers felt should have been caught.

Instead of a routine play, though, Indians outfielder Albert Belle watched as the ball sailed over his head.

Writers covering the game felt Belle had lost the ball in the glare of the sun.

Belle was never known for his defensive skills, but even so, reporters mused, shouldn't he have been wearing sunglasses on that play? Hargrove, in an effort to defend his player, deflected the questions with humor. "The sun was a problem," he conceded, "but not even sunglasses would have helped Albert on that play. He would have needed an eclipse."

Just Following Orders

During the off-season, players will often work out on their own. They figure if they keep in shape during the long winter months, they'll benefit when spring rolls around. Steve Wilson, a southpaw pitcher for the Los Angeles Dodgers, wanted to have a good 1993 season.

Determined to throw throughout the winter, he got permission from the owner of a sporting-goods store to pitch in the spacious cellar of the building.

When the Dodger pitching coach Ron Perranoski heard of this, he had to be pleased with Wilson's initiative. Still, Perranoski couldn't resist the opportunity to fire off a one-liner of his own. "That's not what I meant when I told him he should be throwing inside more," the coach joked.

BASEBALL'S ODD HUMOR

Offbeat Humor

At times, the brand of humor exhibited in baseball is rather offbeat. The wit can be clever, cruel, self-deprecating, wry, almost philosophical, and even a bit baffling. No other game is as rich in humor as baseball. To paraphrase an interesting theory of writer George Plimpton, in sports, the smaller the size of the ball, the better that sport is in terms of possessing interesting and humorous quotes and stories.

To support his theory, Plimpton pointed out there are many golf and baseball anecdotes; some football and basketball anecdotes; and, he added whimsically, absolutely none about beach balls.

Aside from the fact that there are no great Ping-Pong stories, his theory seems sound.

Paige After Paige of Humor

Satchel Paige is one of the most colorful men to have ever played the game. He tossed out funny quotes with the same ease as he threw his scorching fastball or the pitch he called his "bee" ball (because when he fired it, it would be where he wanted it to be).

Paige was a star for an eon in the Negro Leagues. Due to the color barrier, he didn't get a chance to play in the major leagues until he was quite old. How old, exactly, nobody knew. Legend has it his birth certificate was lost, and Paige himself never knew his correct age. The generally held belief is that when Bill Veeck signed him to a big-league contract with the Cleveland Indians, Paige was in his forties. That made him the oldest "rookie" in the history of the game.

As a joke, Veeck even had a rocking chair placed in the bullpen for Paige's use. At any rate, "Satch" was often asked to philosophize on the subject of age. His most famous words, of course, were, "Don't look back. Something might be gaining on you."

But Paige, who once pitched a major-league game for the Kansas City Athletics as a special stunt, at the age of 59 years, 2 months, and 18 days (a record) also gave the world, "Age is a question of mind over matter. If you don't mind, it doesn't matter." He put another slant on the topic once by pondering in Yogi Berra fashion,

"How old would you be if you didn't know how old you was?"

The Berra Brand of Humor

Berra truly was as famous as anyone was when it came to having his own brand of baseball humor. Many of the tales of Berra are apocryphal, but remain classics, nevertheless. One little-known story deals with the time the Yankees Hall of Fame catcher met Robert Briscoe, the mayor of Dublin, Ireland.

Upon learning Briscoe was the city's first Jewish mayor, Berra beamed, "Isn't that great." He paused and then added in all seriousness, "It could only happen in America."

The craggy-faced Berra wasn't afraid to make himself the source of a laugh. Once a photographer told Berra to pose for a picture. "Look straight into the camera," he instructed. Berra thought for a moment, and then said, "Oh, I can't do that. That's my bad side."

Language Barriers

Lou Piniella was an American League outfielder for many years. He was mainly known for his sweet swing and seething temper. Now the manager of the Mariners, Piniella recalled an argument he once had with Armando Rodriguez, an umpire who, like Piniella, spoke Spanish. Apparently the verbal exchange didn't last too long, "I cussed him out in Spanish," said Piniella, "and he threw me out in English."

Language barriers can be a real problem. Fresco Thompson, a famous Brooklyn Dodgers scout, once told the sad tale of a French-Canadian minor-league prospect who couldn't hit a lick. Said the scout, "He's thinking in French, and they're pitching him in English."

South of the Border

Tommy Lasorda was the Los Angeles Dodgers manager until just recently. He had learned Spanish early in life and used that language to communicate when he pitched in Latin America. He also spoke Spanish to many of his players over the years. One such player was Fernando Valenzuela, who splashed onto the big league scene in 1981 with more fanfare than nearly any rookie ever.

Valenzuela, a 20-year-old screwball specialist, record-ed eight straight wins in his rookie season, of which a remarkable five were shutouts. He wound up leading the league in strikeouts, a rarity for a rookie. In addition, the Sonora, Mexico, native went 13-7, winning 65% of his decisions, and authored eight shutouts, also the highest total in the National League.

Naturally, with such impressive numbers he wanted a healthy raise for his 1982 sophomore season. The Spanish-speaking star even held out, not signing his contract until he finally got what he wanted.

Lasorda didn't take the situation too seriously. He was even able to laugh about it, "All last year we tried to teach him English, and the only word he must have learned is *million*."

The Wry "Rajah"

Roger Hornsby was one of the greatest hitters ever to don big-league flannels. His career batting average of

.358 ranks behind only the .367 lifetime mark of Ty Cobb. Hornsby attributed much of his success to his single-minded devotion to baseball—they say he wouldn't even attend a motion picture for fear it would somehow hurt his batting eye.

He offered an opinion why baseball is a better sport than golf by saying, "When I hit a ball, I want someone else to go chase it."

Pitchers' Humor

Another Hall of Famer, fireballing "Bullet" Bob Gibson of the St. Louis Cardinals, was also highly intense. At one time, only Walter Johnson had fanned more batters than Gibson. In 1968, Gibson stunned the baseball world with his microscopic ERA of 1.12, helped greatly by an incredible 13 shutouts. As a student of the game, he once observed, "A great catch is like watching girls go by. The last one you see is always the prettiest."

When Mike Scott and Nolan Ryan were both with the Houston Astros, Scott liked to get an occasional dig in on the aging veteran nicknamed the Ryan Express. One day after a game in which the Astros drew a meager crowd, Scott waited for the reporters to circle him near his locker. Then he unloaded with, "When I saw 1,938 (the number of people in attendance that was flashed on the scoreboard), I didn't know if it was the attendance or the year Ryan was born."

Hall-of-Fame Humor

Some players who suffer through a tough game will boil with anger for hours after the contest. Many veterans, who have experienced years of going through both the good and the bad, manage to forget their fury upon leaving the ballpark. Hall of Fame pitcher Bob Lemon explained why he didn't take his problems home with him after bad outings throughout his 15-year stint. "I left them in a bar on the way home," he offered.

Joe DiMaggio has had myriad honors bestowed upon him. Aside from being inducted into Cooperstown's Hall of Fame, one of his finest moments had to be when he had been named baseball's greatest living athlete in a 1981 ceremony. The Yankee Clipper, still looking lithe at the age of 66, commented with a big smile, "At my age, I'm just happy to be named the greatest living anything."

Odd Source of Humor

For some reason, baseball has been the sport of choice for many intellectuals. Therefore, it isn't too surprising to hear astute words being issued from scholars concerning the game. Perhaps the most famous words along these lines came from Columbia University philosophy professor Jacques Barzun, who profoundly stated, "Whoever wants to know the heart and mind of America had better learn baseball, the rules and realities of the game."

What is surprising, though, is a quote coming from none other than Albert Einstein that displayed a sense of humor and an interest in baseball. It seems Einstein once met baseball catcher Moe Berg. Now, Berg was not a run-of-the-mill ballplayer. He spoke many languages and was truly a brilliant man. Impressed with Berg, the great scientist suggested he would teach mathematics to the ballplayer and Berg in turn would teach baseball to

Einstein. Then Einstein added a sort of humble concession, "I'm sure you'd learn mathematics faster than I'd learn baseball."

Long Distance Calling

When Milwaukee Brewers pitcher Steve Sparks was a rookie, he suffered one of the strangest (and, in a way, funniest) injuries ever. Believe it or not, he actually dislocated his shoulder while, for some reason, trying to tear a phone book in half.

The Brewers trainer, John Adam, came up with the best line concerning this situation. With a straight face he said, "This is one of the freakiest injuries I've ever seen; and a bit annoying because I had to look up a telephone number later."

Painful Humor

Perhaps an even more embarrassing injury took place during a 1989 exhibition game to another Brewer, Bill Spiers. He was in the on-deck circle as a close play at home plate developed. He got close to the action and began signaling to a teammate racing in from third that it was going to be a bang-bang play, and that the runner should slide into the plate. At the moment he was indicating a slide was in order, he got plunked on the head by the umpire's face mask.

The umpire wasn't out to get Spiers. He had simply flung off his mask to get a better view of the play, something umpires normally do. Observers said they had never seen such a bizarre play ever before.

Classic Lines

Back in 1969, a typical diamond brawl broke out during a game between the Montreal Expos and the Pittsburgh Pirates. At the time, Dick Radatz, an imposing and intimidating pitcher at 6 feet, 6 inches and 265 pounds, was with the Expos. Before he joined the fracas, Radatz glared at the enemy.

He then took several quick strides towards his target, Pirate shortstop Freddie Patek. Radatz, fittingly nick-named The Monster, loomed over Patek, who stood 5 feet, six inches and weighed a mere 165 pounds. At that point, Radatz quipped, "I'll take you and a player to be named later."

On February 1, 1985, the Giants swapped Jack Clark to the Cardinals. In exchange, San Francisco received David Green, Dave LaPoint, Dave Rajsich, and Jose Gonzalez.

By the time Opening Day rolled around, Gonzalez had his name legally changed to Jose Uribe. That prompted a writer to observe, "This is truly a case where one player (Clark) was traded for a player to be named later."

Tales of Leather

Two classic stories stand out when it comes to tales of defensive play.

First, a look at Dick Stuart, a notoriously poor-fielding first baseman. The man nicknamed Dr. Strangeglove was a Pirate fan favorite despite his shortcomings with the leather. One day, a bat slipped out of the hands of an opposing batter. The bat whirled through the air towards first base, hit the turf, and then bounced all the way to Stuart. The first sacker came up with the bat cleanly, thus drawing good-natured cheers from a somewhat sarcastic crowd.

When asked if that was the most applause he'd ever heard, he responded, "No, one night 30,000 fans gave me a standing ovation when I caught a hot-dog wrapper on the fly."

Likewise, Johnny Mize could hit a ton, but was a leather liability at first base. When Mize was playing with the Giants for manager Leo Durocher, Mize also became the target of sarcasm. A fan mailed a letter to Leo The Lip which read: "Before each game an announcement is made that anyone interfering with or touching a batted ball will be ejected from the park. Please advise Mr. Mize that this doesn't apply to him."

GALLOWS HUMOR

A Man Will Rogers Never Met

Several decades ago, a pundit simply stated, "Will Rogers never met Howard Cosell." While his quote was terse, the meaning was clear to anyone with knowledge of the old saying, "Will Rogers never met a man he didn't like."

Cosell, a famous sports commentator, was very brash, so the Rogers allusion struck home. While such humor is biting, it should be noted that much of baseball's humor is indeed dark and scalding. Sometimes, though, the humor is not quite that strong, but remains at least somewhat sharp.

Bill Veeck, for example, could shoot off a derogatory line at times which carried the impact of a brushback pitch. He addressed the subject of Walter O'Malley once with a quote similar to the Cosell insult. Veeck called O'Malley, "the only man I know Dale Carnegie would hit in the mouth." Needless to say, these two men stood 180 degrees apart with O'Malley being as conservative as Veeck was liberal.

Ted Williams and Payback Time

It took some time, but in 1955 venerated hitter Ted Williams got a measure of revenge against a pitching foe. Hank Aguirre was a rookie pitcher in 1955, and was naturally elated on the day he notched his first big-league win. Aguirre was further delighted because in that contest he had fanned Williams, The Splendid Splinter.

Aguirre even went so far as to venture into the Boston clubhouse after the game to seek out Williams. Approaching the Red Sox superstar, Aguirre asked for an autograph on the ball he had used for his memorable strikeout. According to legend, Williams stared at the youngster for a moment. Perhaps he even fumed inwardly, but he obliged.

A few weeks later in Cleveland, Aguirre was called out of the Indians bullpen to face Williams once more. Maybe Aguirre was full of confidence based on his earlier success. If so, it was a fleeting confidence. On the first pitch, Williams powered the ball deep down the right-field line; it soared into the stands for a home run.

This was the moment Williams had stored in his memory bank. As he triumphantly toured the bases, he sneered at the rookie on the mound. "Hey, kid," Williams snorted, "go get that ball and I'll sign it, too."

Sparky...

Sparky Anderson is not only one of the winningest managers of all-time, he's one of the most respected and well-liked. Even though he is a kind man, baseball's stinging humor can come from the mouth of just about anyone. Once Anderson scolded one of his Tigers, outfielder Billy Bean, for dropping a fly ball.

While Anderson realized Bean muffed the play because he had banged into the outfield wall, in the big leagues that doesn't always matter. The white-haired skipper showed no sympathy as he met with Bean and informed him, "You've got to hold on to the ball. We have doctors, we have plastic surgeons, but we can't replace outs."

Petey...

The all-time leader for big league hits, Pete Rose, played for Sparky Anderson as a Cincinnati Red. Rose once was peering at teammate Wayne Granger, a relief pitcher who went 6' 2", but with little bulk on his frame. After a moment Rose mused, "He's so skinny the only place he could have won a college letter was Indiana."

...and "Pudge"

Carlton "Pudge" Fisk was so durable he played into his 40's even though he spent much of his career at the grueling catcher position. Fisk was a victim of a line similar to Rose's when he was teased by a White Sox teammate named Steve Lyons. Said the impish Lyons of Fisk, "He's so old they didn't have history class when he went to school."

A's Insults

Two players from the Oakland Athletics came up with scathing insults. First, relief specialist Darold Knowles summed up Reggie Jackson's personality quite succinctly in saying, "There isn't enough mustard in the world to cover him." The flamboyant Jackson was the personification of being a baseball "hot dog" according to detractors and teammates as well.

During the glory days of the Athletics in the 1970s, the team owner was Charlie Finley, a controversial figure. Even though the A's won the World Series for an amazing three consecutive years (1972-1974), Finley was not exactly loved by many of his players. One such player was pitcher Steve McCatty. When McCatty learned Finley had undergone heart surgery, McCatty took this stab at his boss, "I heard it took eight hours for the operation. . . seven and a half to find the heart."

Nettles on Steinbrenner

Like Finley, New York Yankees owner George Steinbrenner is constantly making headlines and enemies. Over the years, more than a few of his players have said they detest Steinbrenner because of his volatility and insensitivity. Some of those players went on to change their minds. Others simply changed their teams, at times being traded due to their public comments concerning their boss.

It should be noted, though, that Steinbrenner, a very wealthy man, is also capable of being quite generous. He must have felt generosity (or a forgiving sense of humor) towards Yankee veteran Graig Nettles because he put up with a lot from Nettles. For example, Nettles once said of his owner, "It's a good thing Babe Ruth still isn't here. If he was, George would have him hit seventh and say he's overweight."

The outspoken Nettles is most remembered for his view of the chaotic atmosphere playing for Steinbrenner's Yankees. "When I was a little boy," he said, "I wanted to be a baseball player and join the circus. With the Yankees, I've accomplished both."

However, when it comes to sheer gallows humor, Nettles threw a low blow when he talked about why a

Yankee losing streak had a bright side. "The more we lose," he began, "the more Steinbrenner comes out to see us. The more he flies, the better the chance of a plane crash." Baseball humor can definitely be cruel sometimes.

Baseball Sarcasm

Long-time baseball executive Gabe Paul followed the 1965 opening of the Houston Astrodome with interest. After giving it much thought, he predicted, "It will revolutionize baseball. It will open a new area of alibis for the players." While outfielders, for example, had claimed for decades that they had lost a ball in the sun, never before had one lamented that he had lost the ball in a dome.

In 1989, when the Indians were still playing in old Municipal Stadium by the shores of Lake Erie, things were quite gloomy. By and large, players didn't like the ballpark. One of the few good Cleveland players of that era was relief pitcher Doug Jones. He succinctly gave his opinion of the cavernous stadium in metaphoric fashion. "It's a museum," he said. "A museum of unnatural history."

The Ryan Express

Oscar Gamble was an outfielder who packed some punch (over 200 career home runs). However, when it came to facing a pitcher of the caliber of Nolan Ryan, Gamble would rather rely on humor than a baseball bat. His feelings on having to step in the batter's box against the Ryan Express were summed up with a touch of sarcasm. "A good night against him is going 0-for-4 and not getting hit in the head," he stated ruefully.

A few days after Ryan had fired a no-hitter against the Oakland A's, the media was notified that he had tossed his masterpiece despite having a stress fracture in his back. When Dave Duncan, an Oakland coach, heard this, he wondered aloud, "What if he'd been feeling good? Would we owe him some hits?"

At Their Own Expense

Usually, the humor that is intended to cause ridicule is directed at another person. However, at times baseball people will aim humor at themselves. A negative, but self-inflicted, barb is not rare around baseball diamonds.

For example, when Jack McKeon was the manager of the San Diego Padres, his team wasn't exactly stellar. For one thing, the talent on the squad was not very deep.

One day while he was sitting in the Padres dugout prior to a game, he noticed some workers were installing thick pads on the bench. With a twinkle in his eye, and a pun on his tongue, he turned to some writers and said, "I told you we'd improve our bench."

Then there was the time the Cubs were in the middle of a one-sided game. They were getting shellacked, so they figured why waste their relief pitchers in such a game. Instead, they employed Doug Dascenzo, who normally was an outfielder, to mop up the sham of a game. Such a practice in a blowout is not uncommon. What made this noteworthy were the post-game comments. A Cub teased the diminutive Dascenzo, calling him a, "true short, short (relief) man."

Dascenzo replied, "Yeah. One inning pitched. Five feet, seven inches tall. You can't get much shorter than that."

Another time, Milwaukee pitcher Dan Plesac was hit hard in relief, giving up seven hits and seven runs in one and a third innings. Somehow, though, he managed to retain his sense of humor when he was later asked if he could remember the last time that he had been hit so hard. He shot back, "Yeah, when I was 12 years old and stole $20 out of my father's wallet."

Sadistic Humor

In June of 1993, the Florida Marlins were about halfway into their inaugural season. Not only did the Marlins have a slew of rookies on the team, even their ground crew was rather inexperienced. While Joe Robbie Stadium was designed and intended for play by the NFL's Miami Dolphins, the transformation of the facility into a baseball park was successful.

However, when a downpour hit the stadium in midsummer, a new problem became apparent. The crew frantically tried to spread the tarpaulin onto the field before the game would be flooded out. Their efforts were in vain as the wind and rain stymied the crew. The opposing manager that night was Dallas Green of the New York Mets, who pointed out that after about 15 minutes of frustration, the situation, "just got to be a little comical."

Ozzie Smith later said this was one of the funniest things he ever witnessed on television. "That was truly an experience watching the manager, Rene Lachemann of the home team, actually coordinating the crew, getting them into position. He had to show them how to correctly put the tarp on the field because the wind was blowing underneath it and it was very tough. By the time they finally did get it down, it didn't do much good anyway because the field was soaking wet then," Smith said with a grin.

Indeed, the more it rained, the heavier the tarp became, and the more difficult the task became. Florida's Jeff Conine was in stitches as he related, "When those guys dumped the water off the tarp and started running with it, and then it got hung up, it looked like about 22 rotator cuffs went out all at once." Leave it to a player to come up with such an image.

More Sadism

During a 1995 baseball game, Philadelphia Phillies relief pitcher Norm Charlton was on the mound. He wasn't in the contest long before he let loose with a pitch to San Diego Padres' Steve Finley that was hit back to him a whole lot faster than it had been pitched.

The liner off Finley's bat smacked Charlton directly on his forehead, shocking everyone in attendance. Observers noted they couldn't ever recall so much blood gushing from an injury. Such a blow had ended players' careers in past cases. Remarkably, Charlton was relatively unscathed.

In fact, he was back at the ballpark the next day joking with the media. "I've had worse headaches than this," said the lefty, who broke into the majors with Cincinnati, where he became part of a wild crew of bullpen inhabitants nicknamed The Nasty Boys. When reporters pointed out that his bruised appearance was quite a sight, he responded, "I guess I'll have to cancel that GQ (Gentlemen's Quarterly fashion magazine) cover."

Charlton even insisted he came to the park because he felt he was capable of pitching even with injuries less than 24 hours old. With that thought in mind, reporters approached the Phillies manager Jim Fregosi. "Would you actually use him tonight?" they queried. Fregosi showed his ability to employ gallows humor by saying, "Why not? He didn't throw that many pitches last night."

Death Wish?

John Kruk was a solid hitter despite the fact that he had a body that was atypical of an athlete. Kruk was listed as being 5' 10" and 214 pounds, so he was hardly trim.

At any rate, when he had to visit Denver to play the Rockies in their mile-high altitude, he naturally had difficulty breathing. Somehow, a huffing Kruk could even take the subject of death and give it a humorous twist. He observed, "I don't think I'd like to play here. I'd die. It's a nice city, but what would I see of it if I was dead?"

Sleight of Hand

More than any other sport, baseball is famous for its trick plays. Some of these plays are rather routine (even if they aren't employed very often), such as the suicide squeeze play or the double steal. However, there are other trick plays which are as interesting and as deceptive as a magician's legerdemain. These plays are the ones that astonish and delight fans.

The Hidden Potato Trick

The selection here for the greatest trick play of all time is a sort of variation on the hidden ball trick. It took place on August 31, 1987, during a meaningless minor league contest. Dave Bresnahan, Williamsport's catcher, and the great-nephew of one of the greatest catchers of all time,Roger Bresnahan, devised a fantastic and unconventional scheme.

He knew the time was right to unveil his plan when a runner from the opposing Reading team had raced home, and another runner, Rick Lundblade, pulled up at third. Bresnahan had been waiting for just such a situation.

So, Bresnahan asked the home plate umpire for a time-out, saying he needed a new mitt. What the runner on third did not realize was that the new glove had a peeled potato hidden inside. As the next pitch came in to Bresnahan, he held the potato in his bare hand. He then intentionally threw the vegetable wildly, like a hot potato, past third and into the outfield.

Lundblade saw the white blur streak by and assumed it was the ball being thrown on a pickoff attempt—after all, how many potatoes does a guy see whizzing around a baseball diamond! So, at that point he naturally headed to the plate.

Bresnahan, of course, was waiting there for him, ball in hand. It was a sort of "Now you see it, now you see it again" bit of prestidigitation.

However, the ump ruled Lundblade safe, calling the play a balk (or an error, depending on which version is being told of this tale). Not only that, the creative catcher was later: 1) ejected from the game, 2) fined $50 by the Williamsport manager, Orlando Gomez, 3) labeled "unprofessional," and 4) was even released from the team by the Cleveland Indians, the "parent" major league club of the Williamsport Bills (of course, the catcher's .149 average at the time didn't help his cause any).

Ironically, two nights later this seventh-place team ran a promotion for its last game of the year. Any fan bringing a potato to the game got in for one dollar. Bresnahan even returned to the park and autographed potatoes with the inscription, "This spud's for you."

He also made appearances on David Letterman's television show and on an NBC pre-game show. He once joked of his fame, "I could run for governor of Idaho."

In 1988, he again visited Bowman Field, the site of his infamy, where the team now honored him by painting his uniform number on the outfield fence. A team spokesperson quipped, "He's probably the only .149 hitter to ever have his jersey retired."

As if to prove the cliché, "There's nothing new under the sun," it should be noted that the same potato play had already been performed a few years earlier by a high-school team. In fact, the coach in this case had actually practiced the play with his kids.

Oscar-Award Nomination

In a spring training game in the 1980s, the San Francisco Giants had Mike Krukow pitching. Suddenly after making a pitch, he howled in pain. The umpire, concerned for Krukow, allowed him to make a few practice tosses. After making the lobs, the pitcher said he felt he could stay in the game.

Krukow's very first pitch sailed wild, hitting the screen behind home plate. The next pitch didn't even come close to reaching the catcher.

Despite his apparent wildness, Krukow insisted he should face the next batter. He did and quickly retired the hitter by using duplicity. That is to say, Krukow wasn't in pain at all. Furthermore, due to the pitcher's theatrics the batter wasn't ready to hit; he had been duped. Therefore, it wasn't surprising when Krukow's first offering was popped harmlessly to the infield, and the pitcher's fake grimace melted into a Cheshire-like grin.

More Duplicity

Catcher Don Slaught concocted a clever play designed for use by outfielders. His play is to be employed when the other team has a man on third base with less than two outs. Slaught said that in such a situation if a fly ball is hit to an outfielder, "He has to pretend to catch it like he normally does, but then basket-catch it. Then if the guy (runner on third) takes off just a tad too early, leaving the base before the outfielder has actually caught the ball, maybe we can catch him." If so, it would be an easy double play for the defense. According to Slaught nobody he's suggested the play to has tried it, but it remains an interesting trick worth trying.

Catch 'Em If You Can

Another catcher, Sandy Alomar of the Indians, came up with his own trick a few years ago. Mike Felder of the Mariners was on first base with one out. As Cleveland's pitcher Charles Nagy fired a ball to the plate, Felder took off for second. He had such a fine jump, Alomar sensed no throw would be good enough to nail the base thief. So, using guile, Alomar intentionally lobbed the ball in a very high trajectory over the infield. He made his throw appear to be a pop-up.

Fans thought the ball had merely slipped out of the catcher's grasp. The truth was he aimed the ball to second baseman Carlos Baerga, hoping Felder would see the ball high in the air and be fooled into thinking a Seattle teammate had hit a pop fly.

If it worked, Felder would scurry back to first or perhaps hesitate enough to even become a victim of a most unusual "caught stealing." Baseball accounts reveal this scam didn't work, but Alomar was using his head by coming up with yet another creative trick play.

Thou Shall Not Walk

In 1995 another Indian catcher, Tony Pena, helped engineer a replication of a very famous decoy. California's Chili Davis was in the batter's box facing veteran right hander Dennis Martinez. The count was full, at three balls and two strikes, with a runner on third.

Pena crouched behind the plate for the payoff pitch, and then suddenly stood and signaled for an intentional walk.

Seeing he was about to be given a free pass to first, Davis relaxed. And, at that moment, Martinez quickly slipped strike three by Davis. The irate batter later stated, "I got suckered. I've never seen it before and I'll never see it again."

Well, if he was watching baseball highlights a year later, he certainly did see that play executed again. On July 30, 1996, Pena, who said he performed this play once with Roger Clemens in Boston and several more times in winter ball, did it once more. This time, the victim was John Olerud, then with the Toronto Blue Jays. Martinez and Pena again worked the con game to perfection on a two-out payoff delivery.

Olerud contended he wasn't fooled as two of his coaches had yelled a warning. "Martinez made a great pitch down and away," claimed Olerud. "It might have looked like I was tricked, but I wasn't."

At any rate, the ironic part of it all is the fact that this trick is extremely famous. When Chili Davis, Tony Pena's victim in 1995, was 12 years old, the Oakland A's pulled it off during the 1972 World Series. It's almost as if Davis (and Olerud?) were proving the axiom that those who don't learn from events of the past are doomed to repeat such errors.

The World Series Deception of 1972 took place in the fifth inning of the fifth game. The A's superlative reliever Rollie Fingers was on the mound, trying to help his team cling to 4-3 lead over Cincinnati. Fingers was clearly in a jam as the Reds had Bobby Tolan leading off first base with the highly feared Johnny Bench at the plate. A few moments later, Tolan swiped second as the count reached two balls and two strikes.

It was then that the Oakland skipper, Dick Williams, went to the mound for a conference. As he strolled off the field, he pointed to first base and said, "Okay, let's put him on." Needless to say, Bench fell for it—after all, the situation obviously did call for an intentional walk. The bat lay on his shoulders as Rollie Fingers slipped a third strike past him.

Seconds later, a job well done, Fingers and his catcher Gene Tenace were jogging to the dugout as Bench stared at the plate in sheer disbelief, a strikeout casualty.

Triple Steal

Just to clarify matters, as touched upon in the "Quotes of the Game" chapter, Herman "Germany" Schaefer was not the first man to "steal" first base. That man was Fred Tenney of the Boston Braves. Back on July 31, 1908, he was leading off first while Luther "Dummy" Taylor took his lead of a few steps off third. Cardinal pitcher Bugs Raymond was the pitcher, and Tenney stole second off him.

On the next pitch, Tenney (five weeks ahead of Schaefer) raced back to first base. With the next pitch he made yet another steal of second in an attempt to allow Taylor to score. Although this attempt didn't work, in a way Tenney pulled off a triple steal by himself!

Hung Out to Dry

Jay Johnstone was a colorful character throughout his years in baseball. Although he was famous for his wild ways off the baseball diamond, on the field he could be quite serious. For example, when he was playing right field for the Philadelphia Phillies he took part in a very unusual and tricky play.

Pittsburgh Pirates shortstop Frank Taveras was the runner at first base being held on by Dick Allen. The Pittsburgh hitter was their pitcher that day, Bruce Kison. It was an obvious bunt situation, so when Kison squared around to bunt the ball, Taveras tried to get a healthy lead off first. Taveras noticed that the Phillies second baseman was shaded fairly far towards the second base bag and that Allen was charging hard on each pitch in an effort to field the bunt. Therefore,

Taveras felt it was safe to try to get an even bigger lead.

He was too bold. When Kison did not bunt the next offering, catcher Johnny Oates saw Johnstone streak from his outfield position towards first base. Oates rifled the ball to Johnstone and Taveras was tagged out at first.Clearly, trick plays such as this can really pay off.

A WORLD OF IRONY AND COINCIDENCE

Only in Baseball

It seems as if ironic events and coincidences permeate the game of baseball. Improbable events occur very frequently. Sometimes these events are wild enough to make a person start believing in astrology. Other times they are merely the type of occurrence which would evoke a "How about that!" from Mel Allen. In any event, they're all noteworthy, to say the very least.

Take this humorous 1988 situation, for example. It was July and the Yankees held an Old Timers Game featuring members of the 1978 Bronx squad versus a group of other older players from the past.

Ironically, on that day an active Yankee, southpaw pitcher Tommy John, was older than every one of the 1978 Yankees. John, an ironman who had his career revived by an operation involving a tendon transplant, was 45 years old.

What Are the Odds?

Joe Niekro was a pitcher for 22 seasons in the major leagues. While he did possess a splendid knuckleball, allowing him to chalk up 221 victories, he was certainly not much of a hitter. Throughout his career, he could muster just one home run (on May 29, 1976). What's so odd here is his only shot came against a fellow knuckleball artist who wound up winning 318 games and who just happened to be Joe's brother, Phil.

Statistical Oddities

On August 13, 1910, the Pirates and Dodgers played to an 8-8 tie. This contest was a tie any way it was scrutinized. Each team had 38 at bats, 13 hits, 12 fielding assists, two errors, five strikeouts, three walks, one hit batsman, and one passed ball. What symmetry!

Another mathematical peculiarity took place in 1941 when Joe DiMaggio astonished the baseball world with his 56-game hitting streak, an all-time record. The Yankee Clipper compiled exactly 56 singles and 56 runs during his remarkable hot spell.

Likewise, another great of the game, Stan Musial, accomplished something unusual during his illustrious career. He banged out a total of 3,630 hits (then a National League record), with exactly half of his hits coming while he played on the road and half in his home park.

Brother Acts

On September 15, 1938, Lloyd "Little Poison" and Paul "Big Poison" Waner hit back-to-back home runs versus Cliff Melton of the New York Giants. Amazingly, it was not merely the only time the brothers, both Hall of Famers, connected consecutively; it also marked Lloyd's final big league homer. In all, Lloyd hit just 28 home runs to his older brother's 112.

For further irony, another brother act was also featured center stage on that same day a quarter century later. It was then that the three Alou brothers, Felipe, Matty, and Jesus, all played in the same outfield at the same time. When that trio took to the field for the San Francisco Giants, it was a first. It also remains the only time such a rarity occurred.

Anniversary Events

Lou Gehrig swatted his first career home run on September 27, 1923. On that same day 15 years later, he hit his final blast. That truly is an incredible coincidence.

Likewise, on September 13, 1965, Willie "The Say Hey Kid" Mays hit his 500th home run. Exactly six years later, fellow longball artist Frank Robinson launched his 500th.

Meanwhile, Eddie Mathews pelted his 500th home run on July 14, 1967. The next year on that day, long-time teammate Hank Aaron reached the 500 home-run plateau. By the way, these two men hit more four baggers than any other teammate duo—even more than Babe Ruth and Lou Gehrig.

More Oddities

Hank Aaron also shares a special day with yet another all-time great, Ted Williams. Both hit their first career home run on the same day, April 23rd. Williams hit his in 1939, and Aaron hit his in 1954. As a trivia sidenote, it was also the day that ace bullpen hurler Hoyt Wilhelm hit his first homer while capturing the first of his 227 saves (an all-time record at one point). What was unique about Wilhelm's poke is the fact that he never again would hit a home run over his 21-year stay in the majors.

Incidentally, since Wilhelm spent most of his years working in relief, there were only two seasons in which he worked enough innings to qualify for the earned runs average (ERA) title. In both those seasons, Wilhelm did in fact win that coveted crown.

More Anniversaries

Then there's Reggie Jackson, who smacked his 500th lifetime smash versus Bud Black of the Kansas City Royals on September 17, 1984. His historic homer occurred precisely 17 years after he collected his first career major-league hit.

Lou Brock established a record for the most career steals (938) on September 23, 1979. Remarkably, that was the anniversary of the day Maury Wills broke the old season record for pilfered bases set by Ty Cobb. Of course, both those records have since been shattered by Rickey Henderson who now has well over 1,000 steals for his career and who burgled 130 bases (in 1982) for the single-season record.

Trivia Oddities and Victims

Moe Drabowsky was the pitcher who surrendered Stan Musial's 3,000th hit. Typical of certain players who seem to have the knack for being in the wrong place at the wrong time, Drabowsky was also the moundsman who lost to Early Wynn the day the great right-hander won his 300th game. Twice Drabowsky had a brush with destiny.

Likewise, Cincinnati Reds outfielder Cesar Geronimo had lightning strike him twice. He was the 3,000th strikeout victim of both Bob Gibson and all-time strikeout king Nolan Ryan.

Harvey Kuenn, a lifetime .303 hitter, was a big-time victim, too. He is one of just six men to make the last out in two no-hitters. Against all logical odds, Kuenn's final outs were both in no-hitters pitched by southpaw sensation Sandy Koufax. The first time this took place was in 1963 when Kuenn was with the Giants. Then, in 1965, Kuenn was with the Cubs when Koufax fired his perfect game.

In a sort of trivia footnote, Roger Craig was the starting pitcher in the last game ever played by the Brooklyn Dodgers, and he was the starter in the first game ever played by the New York Mets.

Iron Men

The next ironic situation involves a chain of events. One, the record for the most consecutive games played was once held by Everett Scott, a Yankee shortstop. He was durable enough to play in 1,307 straight contests. Two, when Scott's streak eventually came to an end, he was replaced at shortstop by a rookie named Pee Wee Wanninger. Three, Lou Gehrig went on to shatter Scott's iron man record as Gehrig played in 2,130 consecutive ball games before bowing out. Fourth, Gehrig, known as the Iron Horse, actually started his streak by pinch hitting for, of all people, Wanninger.

The next day, Gehrig took over the first-base job by replacing a trivia lover's favorite, Wally Pipp. Pipp had asked his manager for a day off, but once Gehrig got into the lineup, Pipp's playing days as a Yankee were shot.

Still More Trivia

Trivia experts love to conjure up the name of an obscure Red Sox player named Carroll Hardy. This career .225 hitter was actually called upon to pinch hit for the great Ted Williams, who hit .344 over his 19 years in the majors. Only eight men in the history of baseball (counting players from the pre-1900 era) hit better than Williams.

What makes the Hardy situation more interesting is the fact that less than a year after he batted for Williams, Hardy also pinch-hit for a young Carl Yastrzemski. Imagine, a light hitter substituting for two Hall of Fame legends.

When Neal Heaton was a rookie pitcher in 1982, he faced Yastrzemski. What makes that worth noting is the previous year while pitching for Miami University Heaton had gone up against Mike Yastrzemski, the son of "Yaz."

Ups and Downs

In 1987, Pittsburgh's Mike LaValliere increased his batting average by 66 points over his previous season's mark. That represented the biggest improvement by any National League player from the 1986 season to the 1987 season. Meanwhile, the worst decline in average over that span was by Tony Pena of the Cardinals. His average plummeted from .288 to .214. The irony here is these two men had been swapped for each other just prior to the 1987 season.

Coming and Going

On September 30, 1927, Babe Ruth propelled his 60th home run to set a single-season record. In that same contest, 531-game winner Walter "The Big Train" Johnson, like Ruth a charter member of the Hall of Fame, appeared in his final big-league game.

It should be noted that Johnson's last bow was not as a pitcher, but as a pinch hitter. Further, as a nice touch Johnson flied out to Ruth to end his 21-year stint in the majors.

A Sense of Completion

When it comes to a sense of completion, consider what happened with Frank Howard back in 1968. Over a torrid stretch of 20 at bats, the Washington Senators giant (6 foot, 7 inches and 255 pounds) smashed 10 home runs. He began his hitting binge versus Detroit's Mickey Lolich. He concluded the spree when he launched his 10th shot over the left-field roof of Tiger Stadium, a Herculean blow, against Lolich, of all people.

Unlikely Events

Vic Power was a journeyman who lasted for 12 years in the majors. He was never known for his speed, stealing only 45 lifetime bases with a season high of just nine. Despite that, in August of 1958 while with Cleveland, he stole home twice in the same game. Not only that, for the entire season he wound up with just one additional stolen base.

Balks are hardly the most interesting of baseball topics. Yet there is one balk which was so unusual it's still talked about. During the All Star game of 1961, Stu Miller, a diminutive pitcher, was on the mound for the National League. The game that year was held on San Francisco's home field, Candlestick Park.

Miller, a member of the Giants pitching staff, was well aware of the gusting winds in Candlestick. However, when one especially strong burst of wind struck him, the 165-pounder was blown off the mound. Since that movement was considered illegal, a balk had to be called on him. What was so odd about that is it was the first balk of Miller's nine years in the majors—and he'll never live it down.

Gridiron or Diamond?

Don Mattingly of the New York Yankees was an outstanding hitter and a fine first baseman. Even before he made it to the big leagues, scouts knew he would be a star. Still, there were several players drafted before him and, amazingly, three of them became professional football stars, forsaking the game of baseball. They were, by a strange coincidence, all quarterbacks: John Elway, Jay Schroeder, and Dan Marino.

Furthermore, yet another college grid star, Rick Leach, was selected ahead of Mattingly. While the quarterbacks had a great deal of National Football League success, Leach was a bust. The only baseball organization which came out of this most unusual draft looking good was the Yankees.

World Series Irony

The same World Series which produced the strange play involving Nippy Jones and his shoe polish was also rich in additional irony. For example, the Milwaukee Braves had their ace pitcher Warren Spahn scheduled to face the New York Yankees in the seventh game. When the superlative southpaw came down with the flu, the starting nod went instead to Lew Burdette.

Call it fate or irony, but if it weren't for the flu bug, Burdette would not have had the chance to win his third game of that Series. He responded to the opportunity, tossing a masterpiece, a 5-0 blanking of the Bronx Bombers. It was "Nitro" Lew's third complete game of the 1957 Fall Classic, and he did it on a mere two days' rest. Only nine men ever won three World Series contests under the best-of-seven format.

Incidentally, Burdette completely befuddled the Yanks, chalking up 24 consecutive shutout innings. That fact becomes rather ironic when you consider that the Yankees had been whitewashed only once all year long. Then along comes the Braves number-two hurler, who shuts them out twice in four days.

For yet another oddity, Burdette had come to the Braves in a trade with the Yankees for Johnny Sain. Sain had been the number-two pitcher behind Spahn for years as was chronicled in the famous phrase, "Spahn and Sain and pray for rain."

There were still more strange events in the 1957 Series. For example, Milwaukee won it all despite setting a record for futility with the lowest seven-game batting average ever at .209. Not only that, but the losing pitcher in the deciding contest was Don Larsen. Exactly one year and two days earlier he had thrown baseball's only perfect game during World Series play. It was a classic case of going from being the hero to being the "goat."

Statistical Oddities

When the 1982 season began, Gaylord Perry, an ageless veteran of 20 seasons, was a member of the Seattle Mariners. At that point, Perry had amassed 297 lifetime victories. Meanwhile, the Mariners as a team had mustered only 290 wins over the history of their franchise.

Christy Mathewson, one of the five original members voted into the Hall of Fame, authored 83 career shutouts. Only two pitchers, Walter Johnson (110) and Grover Alexander (90), threw more. In 1912, Mathewson enjoyed one of his finest seasons with a won-lost slate of 23-12 and a sparkling ERA of 2.12, yet he did not come up with a single shutout. Further, that was the first season in six years in which his ERA was over 2.00!

More Anomalies

In 1962, Maury Wills shocked the baseball world when he established the season record for steals with 104. After all, the previous year he had swiped only 35, and that was enough to lead the National League. In 1963, he slipped to only 40 steals, yet won the stolen base title once more.

In 1979, the 3,000 Hit Club was made up of 16 outstanding hitters. Clearly, it is rare for a player to attain that plateau. Yet on four occasions two men joined that elite club in the same year. That's a statistical anomaly in that eight of the 16 members reached their 3,000th hit in a given season. For the record, in 1914, Nap Lajoie and Honus Wagner did this; in 1925, it was Tris Speaker and Eddie Collins; Hank Aaron and Willie Mays joined the group in 1970; and nine years later, Yastrzemski and Lou Brock reached the coveted level.

Of Ruth...

Babe Ruth went on a home-run tear in 1927, crushing 60 balls into the stands. That total stood as the single-season record for 34 years. The Bambino also drove home 164 runs, hit .356, drew 138 bases on balls, and scored 158 times. Despite all those glowing stats, he was not awarded the Most Valuable Player trophy.

It wasn't a case of the voters being myopic. The apparent snub was actually due to a rule which existed back then. It seems baseball officials did not permit a player who had won an MVP to repeat—they wanted to avoid a superstar monopolizing the award. Since Ruth had already won the trophy in 1923 (although it was then called the American League Award), he could not possibly have won it in 1927 even if he had swatted 100 home runs.

...and Gehrig

Ruth's great teammate Lou Gehrig put up numbers which were basically second only to Ruth's. In his 17-year stay in the majors Gehrig blasted 493 home runs, hit a lusty .340, and piled up nearly 2,000 RBI (1,991 to be precise). For all that production, he earned a grand total of less than $400,000 for his career, pocket change to today's players. Obviously, if he were playing today he'd earn somewhere in the vicinity of $10 million a year.

Grueling Stats

It was enough to make even Brooklyn Dodger fans cringe. Their beloved team went through a grueling stretch back in 1920 that remains unmatched to this day. It began with a May 1, 1920, marathon. The Dodgers played in a 26-inning affair which set a record for the longest game ever and ended in a frustrating 1-1 tie. Incredibly, the next day they engaged in a 13-inning contest, which was followed by a 19-inning grind on the third day. In addition to all that, their 58 innings over that span were played at three different settings, creating quite a demanding trip!

Go Figure

Counting pitchers who performed in the 1800s, there have been 20 men who have won 300 games or more. Exactly half of them never were able to hurl a no-hitter.

Huge stars such as Steve Carlton, Grover Alexander, Lefty Grove, and Early Wynn just could not come up with a "no-no." The combined win total of the ten greats who failed to throw a no-hitter is a staggering 3,268.

Yet, ironically, some little-known pitchers with very little talent somehow managed to achieve this. The most glaring example may well be that of Alva "Bobo" Holloman who threw a no-hitter in his first big league start for Bill Veeck's Browns in 1953. Just a short time later Holloman was gone from the big leagues forever. He wound up with a career mark of 3-7 and an inflated 5.23 ERA.

A Cincinnati pitcher by the name of Charles "Bumpus" Jones actually won less than Holloman (with a 2-4 record) yet also threw a no-hitter. It was his only victory that year and his only appearance. The following season he went 1-4 with an astronomical ERA. of 10.19, marking his baseball demise.

Certainly, George Davis belongs on this list. He had a 1914 no-hitter for the Boston Braves and just six more wins over a mediocre 7-10 career.

Then there was Wilson Alvarez, who was the antithesis of Warren Spahn. Spahn had to wait until his 16th season when he was 39 years old before he managed to put together a no-hitter. Alvarez, on the other hand, came up with his gem versus the Baltimore Orioles on August 11, 1991, as a 21-year old member of the Chicago White Sox.

In fact, a few days before his gem, Alvarez was in the minor leagues at the Double-A level pitching for

Birmingham. Then, in his Sox debut, and in just his second major-league start, he threw the no-hitter.

He was on fire that day, fanning the first three batters he faced to open the game, and the final hitter to wrap it up in style. The Venezuelan left-hander became the youngest no-hit artist since Vida Blue (86 days younger) had thrown one in 1970.

Baseball Humor: Far From Dead

It's really immaterial whether baseball's wonderfully ironic events, rich humor, colorful quotes, and fantastic plays came from the distant past or from the 1990s. Again, despite what pessimists contend, baseball is, and always has been, a fabulously entertaining game. The first chapter dealt with the current decade, so, for a touch of unity, it's time to return to recent samples of great baseball humor. Perhaps this final chapter will even support the contention that many of today's players are better educated and maybe even wittier than players from the past.

Take, for example, an incident from 1997. Detroit's Willie Blair was on the mound versus the Cleveland Indians on May 4th when he delivered a pitch to Tribe batter Julio Franco. The result was a wicked 107-mile-per-hour line drive which drilled Blair on the face before he could defend himself. Blair crumbled in a heap, the ballpark became silent, and Franco was visibly shaken as the team trainer examined the pitcher.

Unbelievably, Blair came out of it all relatively unscathed. He did suffer a "nondisplaced fracture," and was placed on a liquid diet, but he did not have to have his jaw wired. Dr. James Christian, a surgeon, noted, "By moving his head that split second, the ball hit a muscle instead of his temple or eye socket. He was lucky."

Despite the ordeal, Blair kept his sense of humor,

replying wryly, "If I were lucky, the ball would have missed me."

More Injury Added to Insult

In a somewhat similar vein, there was the Scotti Madison injury. He had once pitched at the major league level for the Kansas City Royals, but had since been sent to the minors. Madison became a pitcher for Omaha, the Royals Triple-A farm club.

One day in 1995, a sharp grounder smacked him in the face. The trainer immediately rushed to his side. In an effort to determine how conscious Madison was, the trainer asked Madison if he knew where he was. Madison despite (or perhaps because of) his grogginess, shot back, "Well, I know I'm not in the big leagues!"

A Moving "Violation"

One month prior to the Seattle incident, Detroit's new manager Buddy Bell (in just his second game at the helm) did something no major-league skipper had ever done before. He gave the lumbering Cecil Fielder permission to steal a base and got positive results! After a record 1,097-game dry spell, Fielder stole the first base of his career.

Second-base umpire Tim Tschida, tongue in cheek, observed that the accomplishment was "bigger than Nolan Ryan's seventh no-hitter."

Maybe so, After all, Ryan was capable of hurling a no-hitter virtually any time he took to the mound; Fielder at 250 (or more) pounds was never a threat to run. To rumble, perhaps, but not to run.

As for Fielder's reaction, he wanted to take the bag off the field immediately as a souvenir. He even joked with writers later saying, "I told you I was going to get one. I've been working hard on my jumps the last nine years. The pressure's off now. I'll go from here. Bell might start running me a little more."

After giving that idea a bit of thought, Fielder concluded, "I hope not." In fact, for the record, he ran just once more in 1996 and actually stole another base. At that point, he could proudly tease, "Two career steals and counting."

When is a Sacrifice Fly Not a Sacrifice Fly?

Danny Hocking is hardly a household name. Going into the 1997 season, he sported a career batting average of .205, with stops in more minor league cities than an old vaudeville act. In May of 1996, he was hitting under a "buck," baseball jargon for an average below the piddling .100 plateau. However, he finally found a modicum of success as he hit a sacrifice fly to help his Twins win a 2-0 contest over Seattle.

After the game, in typical self-deprecating baseball humor, Hocking wryly remarked, "I've been telling people I've been hitting a lot of sacrifice flies." Like a fine comedian, he paused for a beat and then added the punch line, "There just hasn't been anybody on third base."

A Mysteriously Moving Ball

Yet another 1996 tale involved White Sox starting pitcher Kirk McCaskill. He was facing the Texas Rangers during an April game. When the baseball began taking some suspicious dips, Ranger manager Johnny Oates got quite upset. He demanded to see the ball, figuring McCaskill was scuffing it to make it move in such a fashion. After examining the ball, Oates commented, "Black and Decker would have been proud of it."

A Brand-New Pitch

Oates wasn't the only man to come up with a clever one-liner. During a Chicago-Cincinnati contest, Cubs relief pitcher Bob Patterson faced the always-tough Barry Larkin. The Cincinnati shortstop took Patterson deep for a 10th-inning, game-winning home run.

Later, when asked what pitch he had thrown, Patterson retorted, "It was a cross between a changeup and a screwball. It was a screwup."

Stand-Up Act

During spring training of 1994, Charlie Hough was pitching for the Florida Marlins and was sounding very much like a stand-up comic. For example, the 46-year-old knuckleball artist had just enjoyed a 2-for-3 day at the plate against none other than the Cy Young Award recipient Greg Maddux.

After the game, Hough teased the superstar pitcher who was coming off his second successive 20-win season, "I don't know how that guy keeps winning."

Shortly after that, on Florida's opening day, Hough walked and singled against the Dodgers Orel Hershiser, who was no slouch himself. In fact, no other Marlin batter reached base more often than Hough that day.

On the negative side, Hough cost himself a run while he was motoring around the base paths. As he scooted from first base to second, Hough was hit in the foot by a ground ball off the bat of Chuck Carr. When someone asked Hough what the odds were of him getting called out on runner's interference, the veteran pitcher responded with incredulity, "Me? What are the odds of me being a runner?"

Hough's hitting and comedy continued. By the end of his second regular-season game he had produced three hits. That represented one more hit than he had chalked up for the entire 1993 campaign. Even though there were only nine players and just five pitchers ever to come up with a base hit beyond the age of 46, Hough, one of those in the elite group, took it all in stride. He quipped about his success, "It's not my fault. The balls hit my bat."

Et Tu, Joey?

Like Hough, Joey Hamilton of San Diego is another pitcher hardly renowned for his stick. As he entered the 1995 season, he was such a notoriously poor hitter he had yet to collect a hit at the big league level. Finally, on June 6th his hitless streak, which had reached 57 at bats, came to an end. It was reportedly the longest hit futility skein ever for the start of a career.

Of his historic hit, a double, Hamilton said with a twinkle in his eye, "I could have stopped at first and taken it all in, but I wanted to get as many total bases as I could. The fans were going nuts." He added, "My next thing is to run off a 12-game hitting streak."

He even joked about his minor league hitting "prowess." He recalled how his first professional hit came on a three-balls-and-no-strikes pitch that he shouldn't even have been swinging at since the manager had given him the "take" sign. The single took place in Wichita back in Class AA ball and was especially noteworthy because he confessed that shortly after the hit he was picked off.

Of his second minor league hit, he stated, "I think the pitcher felt sorry for me and wanted to let me hit one. I have no damn idea who he was—he's probably out of baseball now if I got a hit off him."

A month later, Hamilton drew a significant walk. Normally, drawing a base on balls is no big deal. However, this one ended a Greg Maddux streak of having thrown 51 consecutive innings without issuing a walk. It was staggering to see the great control artist walk Hamilton, who owned a career .041 batting average at the time.

More on Maddux

In 1994, Maddux was almost unbeatable. His final statistics read like a line from Walter Johnson's page in the record book. The Atlanta ace went 16-6 during the strike-shortened season. Not only did he win nearly 73% of his decisions, his ERA glittered at a nearly invisible, league-leading 1.56.

In 1995, his ERA went up—to a still-microscopic 1.63. His record, however, was simply unbelievable as his ledger read 19-2 for a won-lost percentage of .905! Seldom has a pitcher dominated the game as Maddux did in that era.

Frustrated batters showed awe and respect by their actions (often shaking their heads in disbelief as they dragged themselves back to their dugouts after making outs) and their words—consider, for example what Danny Sheaffer said.

First, though, some background. In 1995, Maddux had just gone through an especially impressive four-game stretch during which he averaged just 97 pitches per game. That worked out to an average of 10.7 pitches each inning. Further, over that stretch he walked only one batter. Two of those four games resulted in 1-0 shutouts of St. Louis. Now, the Cardinals catcher, Sheaffer, normally not much of a batter, somehow hit safely in both games. When he was asked if he had ever seen a pitcher better than Maddux, Sheaffer calmly stated that he had. "In Nintendo," he smiled. "There's a guy on my computer about that good."

Feared Fastball Artist

When Seattle's Randy Johnson threw his first big-league pitch back in 1988 as a member of the Montreal Expos, he automatically set a record. At 6' 10", he was the tallest pitcher in the history of the game. Before long, batters realized another fact about the southpaw: He threw about as hard as any man to ever toe the rubber.

One day in the Mariners clubhouse, the topic of firearms somehow came up. Johnson said he didn't own any, but felt that in a way he was armed and highly dangerous. He explained, "I keep a bag of baseballs near the bed. If someone breaks in, they better be wearing a batting helmet, because I'm going to throw at their heads."

Heads Up!

An event took place on May 26, 1993, which will forever rank as one of the funniest and oddest plays ever. Cleveland's Carlos Martinez hit a ball deep to right where Texas Rangers outfielder Jose Canseco, hardly a Gold Glove fielder, was stationed.

From the very start, it was an adventure as Canseco misplayed the ball badly. He resembled a combination of a ballerina and a soccer player as he first pirouetted back on the ball before he "headed" it. That is to say, he actually had the ball bounce off his noggin and over the wall for perhaps the most bizarre home run ever.

Indians General Manager John Hart chuckled, "In my life I've never seen anything like that. I was stunned. I've seen balls hit outfielders on the head before, but not one that bounced over the fence."

Ace reliever Tom Henke later called the episode, "One of the funniest things I ever saw." Being a pitcher, he empathized with the pitcher who was victimized by this

play, saying, "It wasn't funny for Kenny Rogers pitching at the time, but you still see that play over and over again, and it's still funny."

When reporters asked Texas infielder Julio Franco if he had ever seen such a play, his reply was: "Yeah, in a cartoon."

Cleveland's manager Mike Hargrove had a different viewpoint: "It amazes me he didn't go down. If a ball hit me that hard, I would have."

Canseco himself could only shake his infamous head and say laughingly, "Anybody got a bandage?"

A Day of Triumph and Disappointment

On November 5, 1997, an oddity occurred when Baltimore Orioles skipper Davey Johnson experienced the "thrill of winning" and the "agony of defeat." First came the pain. After an ongoing battle with team owner Peter Angelos, Johnson felt he had had enough of the turmoil. To end his feud, he resigned, ending a successful tenure with the Orioles.

Ironically, hours later Johnson was selected the 1997 Manager of the Year by the Baseball Writers' Association of America. In an extremely short span Johnson experienced glory and unemployment.

A Rookie of the Year Who Almost Wasn't

The 1997 recipient of the Rookie of the Year Award in the National League was Philadelphia's stellar shortstop Scott Rolen. The ironic circumstance in his situation involves the fact that he came within inches of being denied the award.

It all started on September 7, 1996, when Rolen stood in the batter's box against the Chicago Cubs and pitcher Steve Trachsel. The right-hander reared back, fired the ball, and plunked Rolen with a pitch. The ball shattered Rolen's right forearm, ending his season.

At the time Rolen had chalked up 130 at bats, which just happens to be the maximum amount of trips to the plate a man can have before losing his rookie status. Had Rolen cracked a hit, or even made an out, instead of being hit with the pitch, he would have been ineligible for the rookie honors in 1997.

Only joking slightly, Rolen accepted his kudos saying, "This would be a good time to thank Steve Trachsel, who was a big part of this. At the time, I wasn't really happy with him. Now, I might give him a call and thank him."

End of a Dynasty

When Rolen won the trophy, it snapped a five-year dynasty for the Dodgers as their rookies captured this award from 1992 through 1996. No team ever enjoyed a streak that long for Rookie of the Year domination. The previous five Dodgers to win the award were Eric Karros, Mike Piazza, Raul Mondesi, Hideo Nomo, and Todd Hollandsworth.

Rolen, who was a unanimous selection, joined yet another Dodger, Jackie Robinson (1947), and six other National League stars to win the trophy unanimously. The others were: Orlando Cepeda (1958); Willie McCovey (1959); Vince Coleman (1985); Benito Santiago (1987); Piazza (1993); and Mondesi (1994).

Unanimity

Not only did Rolen win the Rookie of the Year Award unanimously in 1997, so did the American League winner, Boston's Nomar Garciaparra, also a shortstop. Garciaparra, whose first name is actually his father's name spelled backward (Ramon), sizzled all year long for the Red Sox.

The Rolen-Garciaparra duo marks only the third time both rookie winners were unanimous selections. The other times came in 1993 with Piazza and the American League winner, Tim Salmon of the Angels; and in 1987 when Mark McGwire won in the American League as an Oakland Athletic, and Santiago won in the National League while with the San Diego Padres.

More Unanimity

The most prestigious of all baseball's postseason awards is the Most Valuable Player. In 1997 Ken Griffey, Jr. impressed the voters so much, he won this award by gaining all 28 of the first-place votes. In doing so he became just the 13th unanimous MVP recipient. Clearly, he deserved such honors. He smacked the ball to a .304 tune while banging out 56 home runs, to lead the American League. Those 56 blasts also represent the seventh-highest single season total ever. In addition, he drove home 147 runs, first in the majors.

Not only that, Griffey led his league in runs with 125, total bases with 393, and slugging percentage at .646. The versatile center fielder also captured his eighth consecutive Gold Glove award.

Moving Up Quickly

Thanks to his power production in 1997, Griffey (a.k.a. "The Kid") is swiftly moving up among the ranks of the all-time great hitters. He now owns 294 career home runs, which ranks him #76 on the lifetime list of sluggers.

His pace is quickening, too. On April 25th, he became the fourth youngest player to hit the 250-homer plateau. Only Jimmie Foxx, Eddie Mathews, and Mel Ott, all Hall of Famers, were faster at attaining that level.

If Griffey were to enjoy yet another explosive season next year, he could conceivably crack the top 50 on the list of the greatest sluggers of all-time.

Cy Young to Sayonara?

Montreal's ace hurler Pedro Martinez won the National League's Cy Young Award in 1997 thanks to some sterling statistics. He posted a minuscule ERA of 1.90 to go with his won-lost ledger of 17-8. His staggering strikeout total of 305 didn't hurt his cause, either.

In winning the award, Martinez ended a streak of four straight Cy Young Awards going to Atlanta pitchers. If it weren't for Martinez, the Braves would have won a fifth consecutive award, since the number two and three men in the voting were Greg Maddux and Denny Neagle, both Braves.

However, what is odd about Martinez's victory is the fact that on the day he won the award he spoke of playing on a new team in 1998. And he was soon traded to the Boston Red Sox, to become only the sixth man ever to win the Cy Young Award in the fall, only to move on to a new team by the following spring. The others to do this were: Dave Cone in 1994 (from the Kansas City Royals to the Toronto Blue Jays); Greg Maddux in 1992 (from the Chicago Cubs to the Atlanta Braves); Mark Davis in 1989 (from the San Diego Padres to the Kansas City Royals); Frank Viola in 1988 (from the Minneosota Twins to the New York Mets); and Jim "Catfish" Hunter in 1974 (from the Oakland Atlethics to the New York Yankees).

World Series Oddity

When the Cleveland Indians played the Florida Marlins in the seventh game in the 1997 World Series, they gave the all-important starting assignment to Jaret Wright. What made that so unusual is: a) he hadn't even been on the 40-man roster of the Indians as of the spring of 1997; b) the son of former big-league pitcher Clyde Wright had just climbed from the low minors to the majors, all in one year; and c) his career victory total in the majors was a meager eight (no pitcher in the 93 World Series played had ever started the seventh game with fewer lifetime wins). Despite the Indians loss, Wright pitched well. He had definitely made a name for himself over the course of one highly charged season.

Incidentally, the Indians outscored the Marlins in the Series by a 44-37 margin, outhit them .291 to .272, and outpitched them with a 4.66 ERA versus a 5.48 ERA, yet lost the title to Florida. Of course in the playoffs against the Orioles, Cleveland was outscored yet won the pennant anyhow.

Rip Van Smith

All-time save king Lee Smith announced his retirement in 1997.

Catcher Tom Pagnozzi, a former teammate, recalled a Smith anecdote.

"One time we had a rain delay and he was sleeping in a truck in the outfield behind the fence. I gave him a hot-foot, but I didn't know the guy was that sound a sleeper. The truck almost caught on fire. The best part of it was he woke up, put out the fire with his hat, and then goes back to sleep." No wonder they call relievers such as Smith "firemen."

Gaetti Humor

Gary Gaetti entered 1997 as a 15-year veteran. The St. Louis third baseman was closing in on several career milestones. He recorded his 2,000th hit during the year. He also scored his 1,000th run later in the season on a homer against Pedro Astacio. Gaetti was pleased, of course, but remained modest, joking, "I've probably been thrown out 1,000 times at the plate, too."

A Case of Mistaken Identity

The Atlanta Braves spent part of the 1997 season negotiating a new long-term contract with their superstar, pitcher Greg Maddux. The front office and fans alike were anxious to secure Maddux for the future. Finally, in August, the signing took place, with Maddux receiving a record $57.5 million.

Later that day, during a home contest, the Braves

placed an announcement on the scoreboard to notify their fans that Maddux was back in the fold. The sellout crowd of 47,649 rose to their feet, cheering the good news. A figure emerged from the dugout to acknowledge the applause with a tip of the cap. That was fine. The only problem was the player was jokester Rafael Belliard, not Maddux.

Induction Humor

When Dodger manager Tommy Lasorda was inducted into the Hall of Fame in August of 1997, he retold one of his favorite stories. Lasorda was a member of the 1955 World Champion Brooklyn Dodgers. Years later, he was talking with a Brooklyn teammate, Pee Wee Reese. Lasorda began, "Pee Wee, if I told you one of the 25 guys on that team that year would manage the Dodgers (later) to a World Championship in 1981, you'd put me at number twenty-five."

Reese then disagreed, saying he would have placed Lasorda number twenty-four. At that point Lasorda asked who, then, would've been Reese's last selection.

Reese replied, "(Sandy) Amoros—he couldn't speak English."

A Moving Experience

On May 2, 1996, an earthquake rocked Seattle during a game between the Mariners and the Indians. The shake, which registered 5.4 on seismographs, shook the Kingdome for about 15 seconds. Although nobody was hurt, chaos ruled for quite some time.

For example, the Mariners radio announcer Dave

Niehaus told his listeners, "I think we're having an earthquake. I'm out of here!"

Meanwhile, on the field the two managers, Lou Piniella and Mike Hargrove, were conferring. Piniella asked Hargrove what he wanted to do. The Tribe skipper replied, "We've got two choices: finish the game, or I go back to our hotel and go up to my room on the 34th floor. What do you think I want to do?"

Well, the game was suspended, but even out of potential tragedy came more of baseball's unique humor. For example, the very next day, Seattle's Norm Charlton turned in a zany report. "When I got home (from the suspended game)," he began, "my clothes were strewn all over the place and the pictures were off the wall." He paused dramatically, and then added, "But that's the way it was when I left."

ABOUT THE AUTHOR

Wayne Stewart spent the first 21 years of his life in Donora, Pennsylvania, which happens to also be the birthplace of Hall of Famer Stan "The Man" Musial.

Interestingly, that same small town produced several other big league baseball players, including a high school classmate of Wayne's, Ken Griffey, Sr. Although they were also teammates on the school's baseball team, both being outfielders, Wayne notes he played behind Griffey...way behind him. Griffey was a "good stick, good glove" type player while Wayne was more "weak stick, good typewriter" (he wrote sports for the school newspaper). By the way, Donora is also listed as the birthplace of Ken Griffey, Jr., who, coincidentally, was born on the same day as Musial.

Wayne now lives in Lorain, Ohio, married to Nancy (Panich) Stewart, and is the father of Sean and Scott. Wayne has been writing professionally for nearly 20 years and has sold close to 500 articles to such national publications as *Baseball Digest, Beckett Publications, USA Today/Baseball Weekly,* and *Boys' Life*. He has also written stories for many major league teams' publications, including the Braves, Yankees, White Sox, Orioles, Padres, Twins, Phillies, Red Sox, A's, and Dodgers. He has written for four Ohio newspapers, for a baseball Hall of Fame publication, and also has a story that appears in an anthology on baseball. He is also a member of, and has written for, S.A.B.R. (Society for American Baseball Research).

INDEX